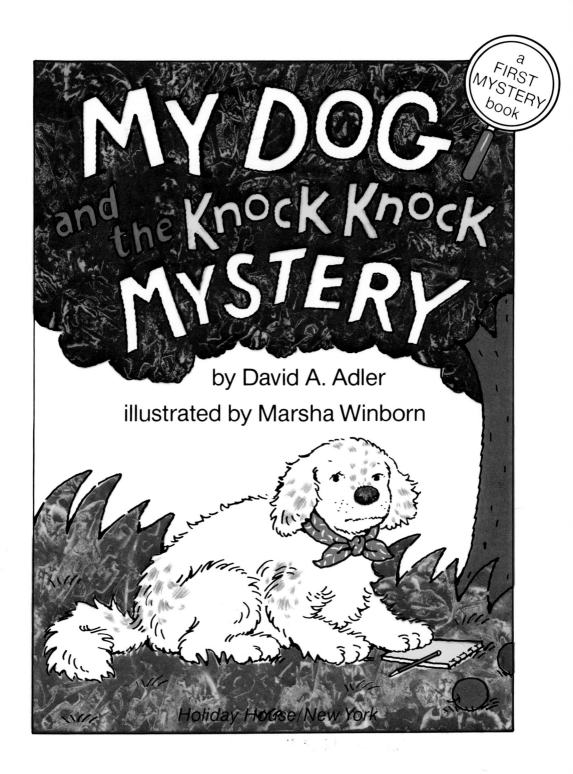

# MY DOG
## and the Knock Knock
## MYSTERY

a FIRST MYSTERY book

by David A. Adler

illustrated by Marsha Winborn

Holiday House / New York

Text copyright © 1985 by David A. Adler
Illustrations copyright © 1985 by Marsha Winborn
All rights reserved
Printed in the United States of America
First Edition

Library of Congress Cataloging in Publication Data

Adler, David A.
My dog and the knock knock mystery.

(First mystery)
Summary: Jennie's dog, who is good at solving mysteries,
helps her friend Billy discover the source of the
mysterious knocking at his house.
1. Children's stories, American.  [1. Dogs—Fiction.
2. Mystery and detective stories]  I. Winborn, Marsha,
ill.  II. Title.  III. Series.
PZ7.A2615Myd  1985     [E]      84-19213
ISBN 0-8234-0551-6

*For  Billie  Goldwyn*

My name is Jennie.
This is my dog.
My dog has white curly hair,
lots of spots, a long tail
and is really smart.
She solves mysteries.
I couldn't think of a good name
for my dog,
so I just call her
My Dog.

One morning
I was sitting on my porch
reading a book about cats.
My Dog wasn't reading with me.
She doesn't like cats.
My Dog was playing
with a toy bone.

I was reading about
what cats like to eat.
They like meat and fish.
Then My Dog poked me with her nose.
I looked up and saw Billy Jones.
He was standing
on the porch steps.
"I need you to help me
solve a mystery," Billy said.

Billy sat next to me.

He sat on My Dog's toy bone.

As soon as Billy sat down,

he began to yawn.

My Dog poked him.

I said to Billy,
"My Dog wants you to tell us
about the mystery."
Billy laughed.
"What does a dog know
about mysteries?"

Then Billy yawned again
and told us,
"I'm not getting any sleep.
Every night someone knocks on my door.
When I ask who it is,
no one answers.
When I look outside,
no one is there."

Billy's eyes began to close.
My Dog poked him
and Billy told us more.
"I hear those knocks
a few times each night,
but I never find anyone outside."
"Maybe it's a ghost," I said.

My Dog barked.
I knew what she wanted.
"My Dog wants you
to take us to your house.
My Dog will solve your mystery."

As soon as Billy and I got up,
My Dog picked up her toy bone.
She began to play with it.
Billy laughed again.
"Your dog is no detective.
She poked me and barked
because she wanted her bone."

"Come on," I called to My Dog.
"This is no time to play.
 We have a mystery to solve."
 My Dog dropped the bone
 and followed us to Billy's house.

Billy's house is small.
I walked around it
and looked for clues.
While I was looking,
My Dog sat under an apple tree.
Some apples had fallen
and My Dog was eating them.
"Come on," I called to My Dog.
"This is no time to eat.
We have a mystery to solve."

We walked around the house again
and looked for clues.
But there were none.
The only footprints we found
were ours.
"There are no clues out here,"
I told Billy.
"We'll have to look inside."

I was about to go into the house
when I noticed
that My Dog wasn't with us.
She was eating again.
"If you keep eating apples,
  you'll get sick," I told My Dog.
"Now come and help me solve
  this mystery."

The rooms in Billy's house
are all on the same level.
I looked around.
The living room was nice and neat.
And it was green.
Everything was green.

"We had plants in here once," Billy said,
"but when they needed water
    it was hard to find them.
    I once watered the couch."
The couch looked like
    it needed water.
    It was beginning to fade.

Everything in the kitchen was yellow.
Billy's room was red.
Then, just as we walked into
Billy's room, we heard a knock.
"That's it!" Billy said.
We ran to the front door,
but no one was there.

"That happens every night," Billy said.
"I'm not getting any sleep."
"Well, it's not a ghost," I said.
"Ghosts only knock at night."

I looked all around.
I looked behind the bushes and trees.
No one was hiding.
I looked for fresh bicycle tracks,
or car tracks.
There were none.

"Why don't you ask your dog
who is knocking on my door?"
Billy said.
So I did.
My Dog barked.
She barked again.
I didn't know what
she was trying to tell me.

"Your dog isn't smart,"
  Billy said.
"She's just noisy."
"Yes, she is smart," I said.
"She wants me to ask you
  when you first heard
  a mystery knock."

"Oh, your dog doesn't want you
to ask that,"
Billy said
as he walked into his house.
"All your dog wants to do
is play and eat."

My Dog and I
followed Billy inside.
Just as we passed the green room
we heard another knock.
We ran outside
and saw an apple roll off the roof
and onto the ground.

My Dog ran past us
and bit into the apple.
"You'll get sick,"
I told My Dog.
She looked at me and barked.
Then she ate some more.

Just then I knew
why My Dog was eating those apples.
She was trying to tell me something.
And I knew what it was.
"My Dog has done it again,"
I told Billy.
"She's solved your mystery."
"All your dog has done,"
Billy said,
"is eat my apples."

I walked over to the tree
and shook it.
Apples fell onto the roof.
I told Billy,
"Your room is right under the tree.
Every time an apple falls,
you think someone is knocking.
The only way to keep
the apples from falling
is to pick them all."

That's what we did.
Billy and I
picked every apple off the tree.

And My Dog ate them.

I hope there are no mysteries
to solve tomorrow.
My Dog will be too sick to think.